Magoosy

To Robin Harry, for so enhancing my life, love C.A.

First published in 2002 by Macmillan Children's Books
a division of Macmillan Publishers Limited
20 New Wharf Road, London N1 9RR
Basingstoke and Oxford
Associated companies worldwide
www.panmacmillan.com
This edition produced 2003 for The Book People Ltd,
Hall Wood Avenue, Haydock, St Helens WA11 9UL.

ISBN 0 333 96124 2 99999

Text copyright © 2002 Christine Morton
Illustrations copyright © 2002 Thomas Müller
Moral rights asserted

1 3 5 7 9 8 6 4 2

A CIP catalogue record for this book is available
from the British Library.

Printed in Hong Kong

Magoosy

Written by

Christine Morton

Illustrated by

Thomas Müller

TED SMART

Meet Magoosy — a stray cat.
A very strange stray cat.
He had lots of funny little habits.

For a start, he never went anywhere
without his tatty old hat. He had a
passion for knitting — tail warmers,
earmuffs, that kind of thing.

And he had the biggest collection
of maps in town.

One night he came out of his cat flap in his flat cap.
He was clearly up to no good.

Look at the map. X marks the derelict house where
Magoosy lives. Y marks Larry's Fish Shop. Z marks the bank.
Maybe you can guess how it all went wrong.

It was the dead of night.
   The moon was like a fingernail, but bright.
      Magoosy's tail went swish, swish, swish.
      Just the night for stealing fish!
   Off he went, down the alleyway.
To what he thought was Larry's Fish Shop.

Swish, Swish, Swish.

GGRRRR!

But next door was a guard dog. A guard dog called Ruff. He woke up in his kennel and sniffed the air.

"Fee, fi, fo, fum,
I see the tail
of a cat on the run!" said Ruff.

Poor Magoosy was scared out of his wits.
His fur stuck out like a toilet brush — and he ran.

Up the drainpipe, along the wall,

up the fire escape, along the roof.

But look! A hole!

A teeny-tiny hole in the slates. Magoosy was good at teeny-tiny holes and he was in there in a flash.

And boy, was it **spooky**.
Sheets lay everywhere like ghosts.
Ghosts lay everywhere like sheets.
"Let me get out of here!" said Magoosy.

He checked his map. Then he crept down the dark, dark stairs — into what he thought was **Larry's Fish Shop.**

There was not a herring in sight.
Just lots of paper and piles of files.
He'd missed the fish shop and hit the bank!

Swish, Swish, Swish.

But, oh!

The smell of fish through the walls! Oh, how Magoosy slavered and mewled and purred in the moonlight! He could smell a million fishy smells, but he couldn't get to them.

"Oh my, swish, swish, swish, I can smell a million, squillion fish!"

Look at both buildings, side by side.
Look at Magoosy, trying to hide.
Look at Ruff's mouth, open wide.

"Fee, fi, fo, fum,
watch out pussycat,
here I come!"

The security man came along with a torch that went click-click. "What is it, Ruff? Burglars?"

He peeped through the bank windows and he saw a shadow that should not have been there.

He reached for the alarm button and pressed it.

Who Who Who?

went the alarm.

We know who it was, of course. But the police didn't. They screeched up in their cars and surrounded the bank. "Come out, come out, whoever you are! Come out with your hands above your head."

Magoosy was scared. He wanted pilchards — not prison.
And it's not easy to put your hands above your head.
Not when you're a cat.

He did his best with his paws
and stepped bravely into the torchlight . . .

The police officers laughed. The security guard laughed.
They looked at his map and laughed again.
"It's only a cat-burglar!" they said.

Magoosy was famous. They took him to the station
and took his photograph. And they gave him a medal —

The Worst Burglar Ever Award.

Larry's Fish Shop became famous, too. People came from far and wide to buy fish and stroke Magoosy's famous nose. Because that's where Magoosy lives now, and Larry lets him have all the fish he can eat.

He sits and knits and eats rolled herrings. And mackerel. And cod and halibut and plaice.

(And scampi, prawns, eels, mullet, sole, pilchards, salmon, sardines, tuna fish, trout and sprats.)

And what more could a cat want than that?